Godzilla B.C.E

In The Beginning

Michael Kramer

Table Of Contents

CHAPTER 1

B.C.E

Quite a while back, About 250,000,000 years ago, the Titanus Gojira species and the MUTOs were at fight with one another, as mammalian creatures were impacted by a Titanus Gojira example's radiation which caused them to transform into an animal varieties that can counter a Titanus Gojira. During the center of a fight, a female Titanus Gojira reproduced an egg securely that arrived at the profundities of the Marianas Channel. Following a million years after the fact, another Titanus Gojira example brought forth and became who we know as Godzilla, just he just began at a level of 110 feet.

He follows the pack of the Titanus Gojira species all through the 5,000,000 years he's survived, developed to a level of 175 feet. With his age now, he can get to the Empty Earth and attract more radiation after all he has persevered, with fight scars and indentations all around his body. Be that as it may, when he goes to a lot further spot of the Empty Earth burrow framework, he gets prompted a novel energy signature, which he takes in, and gains another capacity; the atomic heartbeat. Any remaining Godzillas had nuclear breaths, which dealed less harm. Yet, Godzilla acquired a nuclear heartbeat which yielded more power and is omnidirectional.

From the start, he didn't have the foggiest idea what was happening, yet during fight, he figured out how to release his atomic heartbeat at a MUTO home and a MUTO protecting it, obliterating both. His pack, intrigued, concluded that the time had come to challenge the Alpha of the Titans as of now; Dagon, at a level of 330 feet. After a long fight, with pushing, gnawing, pawing and kicking, Godzilla endured and figured out how to overcome Dagon, and had his spot as Ruler of the Beasts.

Some time has elapsed, with one example biting the dust after one more from different animal varieties. Not very many individuals from the Titanus Gojira species lived up until this point.

Also, Godzilla at long last a grown-up and will remain like that for following couple of hundred million years, has vanquished numerous Titans and pushed them to the brink of collapse. And afterward, a long time back, a space rock hit right close to Godzilla's area, killing 80% of all species on the planet and finishing the Permian time frame.

Streak forward to 16,000,000 B.C., where Godzilla has been circumventing the world to dispose of the opposition, being the MUTOs. Abruptly, that meteor thundered and detonated. Godzilla was there to see it and arose a bomb of fire and emerged into the Brilliant Lord of Elimination: Ghidorah. The Ghidorah species' motivation was to vanquish Planets to reap the energy from the planet's center become a lot greater and a lot more grounded, and obliterate the opposition to get the energy for themselves. This specific Ghidorah had been abandoned yet recognized the close by Earth's Empty Earth, which has a thriving measure of radioactive minerals and pursued it, however Godzilla was there to prevent him from destroying and falling the Earth from within. Their most memorable fight close to the meteoroid had Godzilla getting kicked around Ghidorah and kicked into the opening that was in meteor, and Ghidorah taking off. They struggled each other for predominance for a few thousand years, a few times, with Ghidorah beginning to one-up Godzilla's down significantly more. What was surprisingly more dreadful was that not very many

Godzilla examples were even ready to battle, with a large portion of them either dozing to death or were extremely old and powerless.

Godzilla, alongside Mothra, whom their species had a harmonious relationship for a huge number of years began to shape unions with different Titans, similar to the Titanus Rodan, Titanus Behemoth and Titanus Methuselah. With their endeavors, they had the option to debilitate Ghidorah, however just to make him retreat. Following 5 years of nonappearance, Ghidorah got back to Antarctica, as a method for entering the Empty Earth to reap its center. Godzilla was not going to let him through, as he got through the ice, and he remained among Ghidorah and the entry to the Empty Earth. After a long, hard and cold evening of scars and cuts, Godzilla at last figured out how to drive Ghidorah into a trench and made the ice breakdown with his nuclear breath.

Streak forward to 1,100 B.C.E., in China, the twin priestesses see the new Mothra hatch from her egg as the bygone one will rest and die. Mothra brought forth from her egg, as the Titan, Rodan, rises out of the side of a mountain, where he tunneled into and was resting in. Nonetheless, a MUTO blocked Rodan and both took part in a long fight as a more established and getting through individual from Godzilla's species, Dagon, whom was ousted by

Godzilla, split the two away, with Dagon killing the MUTO utilizing its savage power, which sent Rodan flying. Similarly, as he was going to return to rest, a bigger and more solid MUTO wrecked him, named MUTO Prime, and similarly as Dagon was going to get back up, the MUTO Prime penetrated Dagon with its ovipositors, and escaped before Dagon can go after it. As Dagon swam back to his sanctuary feeble and tired, he laid powerlessly as he nodded off to death.

Godzilla, detecting that one of his last individuals from his species was in harm's way, captured the MUTO Prime and killed it by digging and removing its spinal rope. Also, as Godzilla remained there, observing weakly, Dagon snarled to Godzilla one final time and died.

Streak forward to 478 B.C.E., where Ruler Leonidas intends to oust Persia's top dog, Xerxes, as he carried his 300 Spartans to an edge where they draw and kill the Persian armed force. As they do as such for a really long time, a bulky, huge Titan rose up out of the mountain, Methuselah, who kills the lord of Persia, his collaborator and his military, letting Leonidas and the survivors be on a precipice. They figured out how to live and return to Sparta, having a cheer of triumph. Godzilla showed up, and had a short fight with Methuselah, before he sent him back to the mountains before he can bring on any wild obliteration.

Godzilla detected something different was going on; Rodan had risen up out of Mt. Fuji and was destroying Japan. He released his supersonic shockwaves and supersonic fire shoot on the old urban areas of Japan, yet Godzilla met to go up against him and tricked him to Vesuvius, where he overwhelmed and fixed him in there.

As Godzilla watched his life at the sun, he thundered in peacefulness and swam back to his den.

CHAPTER 2

B.C.E Ghidorah

Quite a while back, when Godzilla initially experienced Lord Ghidorah, they fought for quite a while. Godzilla figured out how to tear a lump of tissue from Ghidorah's left wing, yet Ghidorah thought carefully to remove a piece of Godzilla's side. Godzilla expecting to withdraw, swam back out in Antarctica, while Ghidorah flew some place where it can stink more devastation.

Notwithstanding, the tissue they removed from one another figured out how to breaker, and gleam radiant green, and began to frame appendages, changing and changing into a semi-Titan with a domed head, a gnawing tongue, a spiked tail and enlongated paws. As millennia went by, it began to frame wings and was baited to space by seeing a meteor that had a high energy signature. Thus, the Titan chose to fly into space and pursue it, with next to no other Titan notice.

In Promotion 27, a fire broke out in Rome with a Titan, named Scylla, free and off obliterating the city. Godzilla showed up with perfect timing to catch, overwhelm and make her retreat. The Roman occupants additionally rooted for him. Notwithstanding, Roman head Tiberius Caesar began to uncertainty the Titans, since they were becoming to go after their regions all the more frequently after they begin constructing their pinnacles and walls around urban areas. In any case, his partners advised him to wait, saying that their god Jupiter had sent a portion of the Titans to safeguard us, while his child Mars sent different Titans to rebuff us. Be that as it may, Tiberius was not certain, since a winged Titan was resting in one of their significant urban communities; Pompeii, which was a part for crop reaping.

In the interim, Godzilla was swimming close to Old Japan, yet another Titan, with nearby legends naming it "Yamata no Orochi," the Eight-Headed Draconic Demon, arose out of the side of Mt. Fuji, leaving a huge opening along the edge. Godzilla, believing it to be one more Lord Ghidorah, attempted to manage him, yet was immediately overwhelmed by the gigantic, 155-meter tall Titan. Yamata no Orochi set himself free, wandering around the mainland of Asia to wreck ruin. While Orochi itself was not an Alpha Titan, one of its capacities was sonar disturbance, meaning it can utilize radio frequencies to upset Titans and make them denounce any kind of authority. Godzilla, unfit to find and recognize this capacity in time, was past the point where it is possible to stop the whole-world destroying annihilation that this world needed to confront.

A few Titans were unaffected, as they were in profound sleep or were constrained somewhere near Godzilla, however the ones who just disappeared and remained lethargic for these centuries, caused devastation all over the planet, with Rome specifically experiencing an assault two Titans, the common Scylla, who was one of a handful of the exemptions for not pay attention to Godzilla, and another Titan in Baphomet, who rose up out of the incomparable Pyramids of Giza.

Godzilla accumulated partners from around the world in the range of 10 years, as he did already with Lord Ghidorah. Some battled more than others. Others beat their rivals without any problem. Furthermore, eventually, Godzilla's side won with the Titans either compelled to return to lethargy, or compelled to withdraw, or joining Godzilla's side in fight.

Orochi was as yet an extreme test, with it driving Godzilla into the mountainside ditch he rose up out of and truly overwhelming him on different events. Meanwhile, the Titans had a discussion to accommodate with one another, and consented to remain together to the end. Nonetheless, they couldn't identify Orochi on a superficial level; as a matter of fact, they couldn't distinguish Orochi by any means, and for the following 40 years, Orochi remained stowed away from the world, utilizing the Empty Earth for its potential benefit.

In Promotion 79, Godzilla showed up at the shore of Pompeii, simply meandering around, as the disorder following has halted for the beyond 40 years. Abruptly, 8 necks rose up out of the ocean bottom, and Yamata no Orochi began to go after Godzilla once more, this time attempting to choke Godzilla to death and utilizing its sonar interruption for its potential benefit. Abruptly, the fountain of liquid magma close to their fight began to emit, as Rodan rose up out of the well of lava and went by the two Titans, blowing them from the coastline. As seismic action began to result, magma and liquid stone began to burst out, with Debris covering the sky. Godzilla kept on being steady and begun to draw Orochi towards the coastline. Orochi attempted to choke Godzilla once more, yet with the liquid stone and magma beginning to choke out it, Godzilla figured out how to blow Orochi away utilizing his nuclear breath, at long last thumping it oblivious. Be that as it may, the fountain of liquid magma began to frame an avalanche and it blew Godzilla away from the coastline, taking him out too.

At the point when Godzilla awakened, Orochi stood up feebly, just to get taken out by Godzilla by one more impact of nuclear breath. Godzilla then hauled and swam to Mt. Fuji, where he wanted to kill it and leave its corpse in the mouth of Mt. Fuji. Similarly as he was going to get done with the task, a howling thunder that came as far as possible from the Icy began to call to Godzilla and he followed it.

There was a Titan, that was still under his species, yet looked entirely different, with it looking a lot beefier, however its appendages more skinnier, with a more vault head, lengthened hooks and mechanical, glasslike shoulder-spikes and channels. Godzilla didn't have the foggiest idea where this Titan came from, however the new Godzilla, named Xeno-Godzilla, didn't sit around to attempt to kill it. Utilizing its clairvoyance, he let Godzilla know that he was the explanation Orochi carried on. Godzilla maddened released his everything, except this Xeno-Godzilla was substantially more deft and was more qualified for fast battle. Xeno-Godzilla overwhelmed Godzilla, consuming him with corrosive and tearing him with its hooks and more keen dorsal plates, lastly nopried his jaws open, to complete Godzilla with his own nuclear shaft. Yet, Mothra acted the hero, with her hauling Xeno-Godzilla away. She was dispatched rapidly however, being killed minutes after she safeguarded Godzilla, yet through Godzilla's energy engrossing, Godzilla had the option to get back up and utilize his Atomic Twisting Demise Beam to rapidly kill Xeno-Godzilla before he can bring any longer hardship.

Godzilla actually having a portion of Mothra's energy left, utilized it to leave the Cold. He got back to Mt. Fuji and gave Orochi a look, however Orochi realize that the look implied he was saved yet cautioned, and that he needed to remain here for quite a while. As Godzilla had spent his entire existence up till this second, Godzilla drove out a guide of nuclear breath in win, until imploding and falling into the Marianas Channel.

CHAPTER 3

War In B.C.E

Godzilla, after a long hibernation of dozing until the 1432, at last got up from the Marianas Channel. Subsequent to reemerging, he perceives how much progress has developed and that no different individuals from species are as yet living; he is the final remaining one. What encompasses the southern boundary of China is currently an Incredible Wall. Godzilla was extremely confounded at seeing the wall so a lot, that he got through the wall, just to get across. As he moved toward a close by town, a kid watching from a lookout hollered that a Titan has gotten through the wall. Godzilla, from the outset, was mistaken for the cannons and guns.

However, as they began to take shots at him, and Godzilla, who felt some agony, chose to fight back. Similarly as he was going to breathe out his nuclear breath, the radiance of Mothra showed up before him as well as the twin priestesses. They saw the sign and the two sides finished in a détente.

News spread in the arrival of Godzilla, both outwardly, as he regularly showed up in Mediterranean, and verbally, with the news across land-secured domains in Asia and Europe. In the mean time, in Japan, a ninja who had an extraordinary association with the Titans, on occasion involving them for fundamental requirements, similar to transportation and food lumps, with his katana being a somewhat a squeeze to the Titans, comparative with their size. He was a nearby legend, and certain individuals don't realize he exists. He spends covert as a fencing educator and goes by the name of Shodai Sokogeki. His significant other, whose name was Kimi Saguesa, was a mystic in the town, giving individuals hunches about the world and giving her extraordinary linkage to the Titans.

In Extraordinary England, a high-positioning official in the Regal Gatekeeper, whose name is Arkham Cleric, was a gifted warrior who likewise had exceptional linkage to Titans. Be that as it may, his psyche was contorted, with his clairvoyance taking him to the

Vision of Agony, where he converses with Satan. Diocesan was tortured by Satan until he acknowledged his mystic linkage. He presently have some control over his mystic association, however not through contemplation and resolve, similar to the Priestesses and the Ninja. However, he interfaces him through his consuming contempt and strength. He accepts that this world would be annihilated by people themselves due to every one of the progressive creations consistently and accepts that these Titans need to obliterate for us to return to them.

Godzilla detected this interruption, so at some point, Godzilla showed up at the city of London, with an end goal to attempt to kill this evil spirit had clairvoyant. Yet, because of Arkham Minister being protected in an underground passage framework and a segment of the city of London desolated on fire, Godzilla left, thinking he has at last won. This assault shook across the world, with individuals currently questioning whether Godzilla is the legitimate lord to the world and whether Godzilla has become unfriendly out of nowhere. Minister moved toward the ruler, admitting his capacities to him, yet that he'll drive Godzilla down to England's knees with a multitude of mystics. The ruler obliged, giving Priest, 1,200 men who elected to serve under Diocesan's local army. After a great deal of shouting and torment, the men at long last became clairvoyant warriors, under Cleric's order as well as Satan's.

Yet again godzilla detected this new danger, returning again to England to get done with the task. Before he did, he went to Japan, where the Ninja was hanging tight for himself and Godzilla started to sniff and snarl at him. The Ninja got it and answered with the way that Godzilla simply needed to make the best decision, and that the Ninja went on his back to oblige him. As they swam through a tempest, a multitude of boats chose to show up, with Arkham Cleric in the greatest boat. Godzilla moved toward them, however remained détente. Similarly as he was going to swim back, cannons discharged, which appeared to pierce Godzilla, similar to shots. Godzilla brought in torment, and when on a binge to obliterate these boats. He figured out how to obliterate a couple, with the Ninja killing a many officers on different boats. Be that as it may, Godzilla began to feel weird and began to bring in torment. Godzilla swam off, with the Ninja figuring out how to snare on utilizing his catching snare, and lived to battle one more day.

Godzilla washed seaward off of the Amazon, where Behemoth was wandering near, bringing forth new vegetation and untamed life. Behemoth attempted to take in some radiation into Godzilla, yet it was insufficient for Godzilla to remain cognizant and dropped. Sokogeki, zeroing in on Godzilla, felt that the guns had this mystic field to them that harmed Godzilla not only truly, as these cannonballs are beginning to make his veins become purple, however intellectually, as Godzilla laid in dread and unmotivated. Both the Ninja and Behemoth carried out procedure on Godzilla to attempt to eliminate the cannonballs, with Behemoth opening the injury so Sokogeki can eliminate it. He then, at that point, delicately got every one out, with a mix of his sword, snare and strength. Godzilla, recapturing cognizance, expressed gratitude toward both Sokogeki and Behemoth.

Godzilla searched out a Full scale Assault on the armada, with Sokogeki joining his side and helping him. Nonetheless, Behemoth demanded that they need more fortifications. Godzilla called his kindred Titans, Rodan, Mothra and Na Kika, with Methuselah accepting his call, just not showing up in time. Sokogeki connected himself to Kimi Saguesa, saying that they need to carry the Japanese maritime armada to help Godzilla. In any case, with them having lost a conflict against Korea, their maritime armada was at a negligible. Furthermore, Saguesa let him know that the sovereign wouldn't pay attention to a lady from a close by town. Thus, Sokogeki chose to move toward the Ruler of Japan himself and attempt to persuade him. Godzilla obliged, with him flagging the Titans to remain in the Amazon and sit tight for him, while he sends Sokogeki to Japan.

Arkham Minister, learning of the disclosure through his mystic scouts, concluded that he'll control the Titans that are not on Godzilla's side. He went forward, having Scylla, Tiamat and Amhuluk to push Godzilla down to the brink of collapse. Ninja Sokogeki stooped before the Sovereign, with the last option being shaken by the actual sight of him. Sokogeki lets him know that another conflict will happen. Also, that the military should reach out and get to England. The Ruler obliged, with his apprehension gripping from him simply taking a gander at the otherworldly ninja, however noticed that it'll require a long time to get to the Atlantic. Sokogeki let him know that Godzilla will lead them the way.

As they went through days adrift, they understood that they simply had to stand by one more week to get to London. Notwithstanding, Tiamat blocked them and sank 2 boats. Godzilla snatched Tiamat, however at that point Tiamat began to choke him. Rodan and Mothra plunged down to help him however at that point pulled out because of an ear-assaulting signal from the English Clairvoyant Armed force, and subsequently couldn't assault and can thrash in that frame of mind in torment. Tiamat figured out how to drag Godzilla submerged too, endeavoring to stifle him with his constrictive power, yet after a barrel roll from Godzilla and some help from Na Kika, he figured out how to crush out and shoot Tiamat with his nuclear breath, thumping it oblivious. When Godzilla reemerged, he saw his two flyer accomplices in torment. An impact of nuclear breath to the sky, which undulated in the mists and which made the sky shine, brilliant figured out how to assist them with recapturing center.

Following seven days of movement, cannonballs lit to fire at the harbor, both from the land and the ocean. Shodai Sokogeki told his significant other one final farewell until he head off, utilizing his snare and sword. He took a large number of projectiles. Blade wound after blade cut, yet figured out how to arrive at the last level. Arkham Priest was hanging tight for him, with a cutting edge in his grasp. He hollered at the Ninja, "How about we finish this!" And the two battled with Sokogeki taking a bigger number of blows than Minister. After a cut on his leg, Sokogeki tumbled to his knees. Similarly, as Priest was going to follow through with the task, Sokogeki utilized a secret folding knife he had and flung it at Diocesan, penetrating his eye. In the wake of exchanging more blows with their blade, the two sides end with a wound, with Priest missing Sokogeki's chest and cutting his arm, and Sokogeki cutting his head and pushing up to slice the head down the middle, for the last time, at last killing Arkham Minister. After Priest's demise, the Lord and the military restored their cognizance and continued to go after the rebel Titans, as opposed to Godzilla, as they found in a dream signal sent by Kimi Saguesa.

Godzilla fought Scylla and Amhuluk, with the assistance of Mothra and Rodan, and Tiamat re-showing up with Na Kika and Behemoth battling him. Godzilla's side of 5 individuals immediately overwhelmed the 3. However at that point as Minister's body laid there close to

Sokogeki's injured body, a dark cloud showed up, with Godzilla seeing it from a remote place as he powers Scylla, Amhuluk and Tiamat down to their knees. The cloud appeared into Bagan, the Devilish Dread Monster.

Bagan effortlessly took Rodan and Mothra out of the battle utilizing his savage strength and its "Jewel Shard Tempest" which shoots a hurricane loaded up with shards of metal, destroying their skin. As the 3 previous foes went after Bagan out of dread and adrenaline, yet figured out how to dispatch and make them escape, utilizing his "Cremation Laser Horn," a laser which, instead of detonating, consumes the rival with its outrageous speed and temperature. Godzilla, Behemoth and Na Kika were the lone survivor on the field, and they charged at Bagan and gave it a decent battle, yet eventually, Bagan was the person who wins, overwhelming even Godzilla.

Similarly, as Bagan left Godzilla for dead, cannonballs and mounted guns began taking shots at Bagan, with Sokogeki helping them as well.

Bagan, perceiving that the ninja was the justification for the connection among man and beast, annihilated the boat wherein Sokogeki was on and gotten him. Bagan threw him to the inlet, so hard that the wooden dock broke. As Sokogeki got up, Bagan utilized his Plasma Charge Bar on Sokogeki, which the last option attempted to hold him off energetically, both genuinely with blade and profoundly with his mystic psyche. Godzilla got back up, yet observed weakly as Sokogeki was going to bite the dust, but before he did, Sokogeki told him that "You, Godzilla, will be the key to co-existence, not me. Help them learn," and was quickly incinerated to flames. Bagan, now having accomplished goal in turning humanity's back on the Titans, now used his wing-like rocket boosters to flee into space. Godzilla roared out in pain and loss, and with the Japanese having lost Godzilla's closest human ally, they all started shooting their cannonballs at him. Godzilla, while reeling in pain, sought out forgiveness and left them without consequence.

GODZILLA B.C.E

It was 1452, where Saguesa was a priest at the local shrine. When she arrived at the seashore, where Sokogeki's grave was, she saw Godzilla laying there. She telepathically linked herself and Godzilla told her that humanity turned her back on him. Saguesa told Godzilla to not worry, that "we can one day come together after we fall apart." Godzilla growled at Saguesa in physical form, gave her one last look, until he swam back out into the sea.

CHAPTER 4

Godzilla '94

Some place in the frosty waters off Gold country, a rescued boat is recovering reactor centers unloaded there by the Soviet Association during the Virus War. Something turns out badly and a mammoth blast obliterates the boat. On shore, the snow bursts into flames and a cleft opens up, overflowing out steaming heaps of what gives off an impression of being blood. A U.S. government researcher called Keith Llwellyn is traveled to the site to examine the episode, abandoning his significant other Jill Llewellyn and girl Tina Llewellyn behind.

Fighters cart away whole barrels of the 'blood', which upon assessment looks like just amniotic liquid. After showing up, Keith and a couple of different

23

researchers find Godzilla in the sinkholes, where the 'blood' was overflowing off from. The beast stirs and inadvertently kills Llwellyn and the remainder of the examination group. Godzilla then goes after the Japanese Kurila islands. An enduring angler refers to the beast as "Godzilla", subsequent to remembering him from an old Japanese legend.

After twelve years, cryptozoologists Aaron Vaught, a top rated creator and his collaborator Marty Kenoshita, slip into a psychological medical clinic in Japan to meet with the angler, and the angler shows them pictures he drew of Godzilla secured fighting with another beast. The tactical police then, at that point, show up and secure Vaught and Kenoshita.

Some place in Kentucky, a meteor collides with lake 'Apopka'. In Massachusetts, the U.S. military has laid out the St. George project, a highly confidential venture to track down Godzilla. Jill Llewellyn is the undertaking's chief. Vought is welcomed on board to assist with tracking down Godzilla, in spite of that Jill doesn't support the thought. In the mean time, back in The Frozen North, another army installation was built where Godzilla was first found. Then, at that point, a bizarre light was seen enlightening from a formerly unseen cavern, fanning out from Godzilla's cells.

GODZILLA B.C.E

In lake Apopka, the odd bio-metallic meteor starts to mix, moving through the residue like a mass of fluid metal. The test enters a cavern and retains an entire settlement of bats, making 12-foot wingspan animals called test bats. Vaught, Llewellyn and Kenoshita fly to the office in Gold country where the amniotic liquid has started to stream again in the cave. Vaught then demanded this was the legitimate time for Godzilla to be enlivened, however the rescued boat disturbed things and delivered them early. The side cavern is fixed with unusual natural designs, leftovers of an old society with cutting edge bio-innovation. Nobody sees a little animal strike Marty Kenoshita and cover into his neck, even Kenoshita doesn't feel the animal tunneling into his neck. Occasions progress in Kentucky, as unusual occasions happen.

In the Pacific, Godzilla is accounted for swimming towards San Francisco, where the St. George project is laid out at the methodology. Llewellyn and Vought before long show up however Kenoshita turns out to be sick and is raced to a clinic. The naval force is the dispatched to counter Godzilla. After a devastating loss, the tactical thinks about utilizing a little atomic gadget to obliterate the beast, yet Vought prompts against it. He feels that Godzilla is a living atomic reactor, and that the thing the beast inhales isn't fire however something that ionizes oxygen so incredible it transforms it into heat. Llewellyn further proposes that the amniotic liquid was not food as recently assumed, however a sedative to keep Godzilla sleeping. The liquid is hurriedly spread at the mouth of San Francisco Cove. Godzilla swims solidly into the slick fluid and implodes on the southern furthest point of the Brilliant Door Extension.

The military gets the oblivious Godzilla and carriers him back to the St. George project in Massachusetts, where he is housed in a colossal overhang. Tina understands that her mom has been attempting to chase and kill Godzilla for the beyond twelve years. She fought that the beast is only a power of nature, not liable for the harm he causes. Not wishing to pay attention to this perspective, Jill sends her little girl to remain with her auntie in New York. At a military clinic, the bizarre disease Kenoshita has deteriorates, consuming his inward organs and leaving his face dead and with eyes completely dark. Before he kicks the bucket, Kenoshita lets Llewellyn know that he has been taken over by an old power. The power has told him of his set of experiences and the danger that has come to Earth: an outsider human advancement that sends tests to help its colonization of the universe. These tests consume the local existence of the objective world and make an Armageddon monster from the hereditary material. When the outsiders show up, the test would have cleared out all the existence on The planet. An old Earth human advancement averted these tests by creating Godzilla from the dinosaur qualities. Godzilla would stir when the tests showed up and annihilated them before they could replicate.

In Kentucky, the test bats keep on retaining creatures, getting back to the cavern with their hereditary assortments to convey to the primary mass of the test, which is gradually beginning to take on a conclusive structure. Vaught, after hearing Kinoshita's story, reasons that Godzilla was set out toward Kentucky, where the meteor crashed. Be that as it may, before he could show up, he was surprised in St. Louis, Missouri, where another beast arose. Vaught closed to be Godzilla's subspecies, where it was more deft and lithe, yet to the detriment of strength and capability. He named it "Zilla," guaranteeing it to be mediocre compared to Godzilla, and to quickly lose. At the point when the two conflicted close to St. Louis, Zilla really began to outmaneuver Godzilla, utilizing tunneling strategies to divert, snare and befuddle Godzilla occasionally. Nonetheless, Zilla was gotten by Godzilla by a step to the tail, and was mercilessly beaten to approach passing. Godzilla, remembering it as one of his own, chooses to save the monster, and proceeded with its frenzy towards Kentucky.

Nearby vendor Nelson Deride drives Vought to the lake. The two men wear scuba stuff and plunge into the water. They find a passage driving upwards from the lower part of the lake that leads them into a progression of caverns. Vought is scared when he sees a monster paw. The paw is connected to the recently framed shape the test has expected. The beast has the body of a jaguar, the colossal wings of a bat and a hydra-headed tongue made out of snakes. The test has turned into the Griffin, of the Japanese angler's drawings. Ridicule inadvertently bangs his air tank against the cavern wall. The sound then, at that point, stirs the torpid Griffin, and the men quickly retreat however the beast seeks after them. As they surface, they appears to be protected. Unexpectedly the water stirs and the Griffin arises high up. The Griffin takes off and heads to Harrisburg, Virginia.

The beast obliterates a train and an impact fuel capacity tank with energy shots, killing many individuals all the while. In spite of the plunge of amniotic liquid being given to him, Godzilla stirs, annihilating the shelter and slipping into the Atlantic. Obviously he has detected the Griffin's enlivening. It is subsequently resolved that the two beasts will run into one another in New York. Jill attempts to advance into the city to save Tina amidst the clearing. She is caught in the Sovereigns Midtown

Passage when Godzilla steps on it, however figures out how to swim to somewhere safe. Jill finds her little girl as the Griffin shows up and draws in Godzilla in fight. The Griffin assaults Godzilla from the sky, driving the dinosaur once again to the shore. Godzilla loses at first on the grounds that a tank loaded up with the amniotic liquid is as yet connected to his neck, yet Mock and Vought figure out how to obliterate the tank. Be that as it may, Godzilla, actually debilitated, can't overwhelm the battle any more against Griffin. What's more, to a shock, Zilla held Griffin supported with his flaring nuclear breath and paralyzed it for some time. The two collaborated against the winged beast, with Zilla ripping at it and destroying its wings, with Godzilla handling the completing blow with a charged nuclear breath. Triumphant, Godzilla and Zilla thunder, as the two structure a shared regard for each other to head out in a different direction. Contender jets start to go after the two beasts, however Jill Llewellyn cancels them lastly finds some peace with Keith's demise and excuses Godzilla. Jill, Tina, Vought and Ridicule watch from the shore, as Godzilla and Zilla head out in different directions and vanish into the sea.

CHAPTER 5

Son Of Kong

Ruler assembles a group to find any Pinnacle individuals engaged with the production of Mechagodzilla. One of them was Ernest Denham, who filled in as a coder for the Mechagodzilla's computer based intelligence. Denham hurried his stuff and left his significant other with a note, that he was leaving the spot for some time for an outing with his companions. As he hurried down the interstate, a Smack van went by him. Denham, thinking he got away, dialed back to the standard turnpike speed. Be that as it may, the van turned around and began pursuing Denham. Denham called his companion, Peter Englehorn, to set up the boat to get away. Englehorn went along and began to prepared the boat. During the thruway pursue,

Official Theodore Rossius requested back-up to get and pursue Denham.

Englehorn's companions, Carl C. Cooper and Jason McGarvey, needed to follow along on this experience. They let them know that remaining at home was extremely exhausting, and that they told their work supervisors that they'll be having some time off for some time. Englehorn invited them in, with Denham surging in. Denham scarcely made the boat, before the men could contact them. The Specialized squad had a go at gunning the boat and breaking its motor, however at that point it was unaffected by the shots. Thus, the four figured out how to get away. Notwithstanding, the slugs broke tossed the fuel tank, which permitted a path to be completely finished and left the boat that Denham and his team abandoned close to the now obliterated Skull Island, with a tropical storm resulting it. They began to get maneuvered into the island by means of its waves and wind, where Denham and the team took cover inside and attempted to direct it through the island and get in securely. The cruel lightning and wind took the boat and its group down and out. When they awakened on shore, the island was all the while being overwhelmed by downpour, wind and lightning. They got their ammo and gone out in look for cover for warmth and stowing away.

GODZILLA B.C.E

They found a cavern where it lead to an underground passage framework, open from one of the bombs in 1973. At the point when they went in more profound, then found a monster primate incased in ice, estimating at 25 meters tall. They utilized a flamethrower to liquefy the ice, and a rocket launcher to loosen things up. The gorilla fell on his side, still oblivious. Denham simply needed to let the gorilla be, and the remainder of the group followed, however not before McGarvey infused the primate with a portion of caffeine for an endeavor to awaken the chimp. As they go in more profound into the cavern, they feel a strong measure of power pushing down on them. Cooper says that gravity is pushing them harder while they keep on going further into the cavern. However at that point a pack of Skullcrawlers endeavored to pursue them, however at that point the gorilla got them and flung some of them into a gorge and breaking another's jaw, as well as squashing one's head with a monster rock.

During this, Official Rossius utilized the boats that endured the tempest and amassed the blustery island. They let the higher-up authorities know that they will catch them for cross examination. Yet, similarly as he settled on the decision, a multitude of monster bats showed up at the scene. The military endeavored to destroy them, with a considerable lot of them being eaten. Rossius requested to fall back, with 18 individuals dead and handfuls more harmed. In the interim, the pack on the island followed the gorilla as they arrived at a profound gorge with no scaffold to the opposite side. Denham told the pack it seemed as though Kong yet couldn't tell especially in light of the fact that it was so dull thus enormous. One more multitude of monster bats showed up yet the gorilla smacked them away. They got on the gorilla as, through an electric lamp, saw that Kong tracked down a plant and chose to involve it as a rope to swing across. They held and saw an all around light. At the point when the light radiated on the primate, Denham currently at last saw that it was a Kong.

Kong opened the cavern entryway and the light diminished down out of nowhere. It was on the grounds that there was a foreboding shadow which shut out what Denham called "The Moon of this Cavern." Many multitudes of bats showed up, with Kong effectively smacking at them, yet entirely sometimes absent. Be that as it may, there was another adversary available for him. A Camazotz shows up from the mists, with another Camazotz following it. Kong attempts to fend it off, however is immediately overwhelmed by the two and had to the ground. In any case, Kong snatched a rough point of support that was right close to him and slammed it on a Camazotz head, staggering close to its accomplice.

After a great deal of flying, roof dropping and colliding with walls, Kong figures out how to at long last kill one by skewering it with a stone spike from the roof of the cavern room. The leftover Camazotz captures it yet Kong climbs a wall and leaps crazy and grounds an overwhelming hit to the head. The Camazotz withdrew to an entry by the presence of a wormhole. Kong peered down at the opening and hopped into the opening, however not subsequent to getting Denham and the group to hop into it. Kong supported them securely, while taking the blow from the wormhole. Denham and the team fall into the dull Empty Earth, with Cooper figuring out how to snatch a parachute from his pack and get everybody, individually. Kong handled a piece generally on the World's floor yet figured out how to disregard it in a matter of moments. In there, the grown-up Kong is as of now laying down with the adolescent Kong going nearer to it. Nonetheless, a boisterous shriek stirs the grown-up Kong, and Kong thunders and erupts. He sees the adolescent and notification no other person nearby, thus he takes him in. In any case, the Camazotz from the cavern went after the two, however with the strength of two Kongs, figured out how to overcome the excess Camazotz.

Denham and the group seize a HEAV and leave. As they say farewell to little Kong, they fly back, crossing the tactical's boats with a major grin all over. What's more, the two Kongs are there together, in a dad and-child harmony.

CHAPTER 6

Son Of Godzilla

On the distant Soul Island in the Pacific Sea, a group of Ruler researchers, drove by Dr. Michael Sun, is embraced a weather conditions controlling examination, expecting to permit humanity to develop food in beforehand unsatisfactory environments and possibly finishing widespread starvation. As the researchers are drawing nearer to doing the analysis, they start seeing weird radio obstruction that is unfavorably influencing their gear. At some point, a plane flies over the island, and a man utilizing a parachute leaps out of it. At the point when Sun and his aides Christopher Banks and Nicholas Tatopoulos go to explore, the man basically waves at them and goes with them back to their base. He presents himself as Kyle Connor, a specialist who needs a scoop on the researchers' trials. As the investigation is intended to be highly classified, the researchers reject, however they choose to permit Connor to remain with them on the condition he help cook and clean and go about as the group's picture taker. Afterward, while he is investigating the island, Tatopoulos sees a delightful local young lady swimming in the waters simply off the island. At the point when Tatopoulos attempts to photo her, she rapidly plunges under the water and vanishes.

In the long run, the examination is prepared to start. Weather conditions Control Cases on the island start showering a cooling gas high up, while an inflatable conveying a Radioactivity Sonde is sent off into the environment. At the point when Sun is cautioned to remain inside before the Sonde detonates and starts cooling the island, he looks for the local young lady to caution her about the examination. At the point when Sun neglects to see as her, he is compelled to withdraw back to the base. The examination is advancing typically, until the radio impedance returns and the Radioactivity Sonde rashly explodes in the air, setting off an outrageous intensity wave, went with extreme radiation storms. Following half a month, the tempests stop, and Endlessly sun leave the base and start noticing the harm. As they meander across the island, they notice that a settlement of Scylla rise up out of the ground. The Scylla crush the egg with their hooks until it tears open and uncovers Minilla, a child Godzilla. Before long, Godzilla surfaces at the island and starts coming shorewards to protect the newborn child. Godzilla arrives at the Scylla, and quickly goes after them. Godzilla figures out how to kill one close by to-hand battle, then, at that point, kills one more with his nuclear breath. The last Scylla bounces away, leaving Minilla free from any potential harm. The local young lady approaches Minilla and throws organic product into his mouth, yet is compelled to escape when Godzilla approaches the newborn child. Godzilla permits Minilla to take hold of his tail, and conveys him up a slope.

One evening, Sun and the researchers find the local young lady taking one of Sun's shirts, however she escapes before they can get her. Sun finds her to a cavern on the island, however slips and is thumped oblivious. At the point when the young lady gets back to the cavern, she holds a blade to Sun and blames him for being a cheat attempting to take her note pad. Sun guarantees her he isn't a criminal, and is essentially attempting to recover his shirt, yet he chooses to let her keep it. The young lady presents herself as Gwen Mary Watson, the girl of a dealt with the researcher island and kicked the bucket a long time back. Sun takes Gwen back to the camp and acquaints her with the others. At the point when Godzilla passes by and obliterates the camp, Gwen offers the researchers home in her cavern. Following a couple of days, large numbers of the researchers start showing side effects of an extreme fever, which Gwen perceives as "Soul Fever." She says the main fix is warm red water from a bubbling lake situated on the inside of the island. Gwen and Sun set off, and as they head toward the lake they disregard a valley, which Gwen cautions is the "Valley of the Alpha Scylla," a superspecies plunge of the Scylla. At last they arrive at the lake, yet find that Godzilla and Minilla have taken up home close to it. Gwen comments that Godzilla is "instructing his child." Godzilla endeavors to show Minilla how to inhale nuclear breath, yet finds he can inhale desolate smoke rings. Godzilla tramples Minilla's tail, which makes him regurgitate an impact of fire from his mouth. Godzilla praises his child, who yells enthusiastically at his prosperity. Gwen figures out how to gather a portion of the water, and takes it back to the cavern. She oversees the water to the men, and they rapidly recuperate.

One day while Gwen is gather tooing plants on the island, she is gone after by a Scylla, and she shouts to Minilla, who acts the hero. While Minilla attempts to fend off the Scylla, he coincidentally kicks a stone into an Alpha Scylla's valley, which stirs the giant insect. At the point when the Scylla hears Godzilla drawing nearer, it takes off. Gwen attempts to get back to the cavern, however she is gone after by the Alpha Scylla. Connor sees Gwen and attempts to get her to somewhere safe and secure, yet they are cornered by the Alpha Scylla, who starts spitting webbing at them. Connor utilizes his lighter to slice through the Alpha Scylla's web, and he and Gwen effectively get away from back to her cavern. Notwithstanding, when they are in the cavern, they observe that the Alpha Scylla is holding up outside and catching them inside with webbing. Gwen and Connor get away from the cavern from a mysterious submerged exit, and effectively set up a radio recieving wire outside the cavern, permitting Banks to connect with Ruler, who send a salvage chopper. Sun says that they have no desire for getting away bursting at the seams with the beasts meandering the island, and suggests that they direct their weather conditions explore once more and freeze the beasts. The others concur, and they promptly start arrangements.

In any case, Ruler ran into an issue as Colonel Diane Encourage and Jackson Barnes, two individuals from the salvage mission, were being pursued by maverick contender jets. They reached William Stenz and his more youthful sibling Alexander Stenz, to send more warriors. Yet, they've been subverted by Titan-Rise, the authority name of the eco-fear mongers that Alan Jonah worked for. Dr. Jack Stane, who likewise worked in the Air Power, proposed to fly the last contender fly leftover, and pursued down the planes killing the chopper. The arrangement worked and the salvage mission had the option to continue according to plan.

Minilla approaches the cavern to attempt to safeguard Gwen from the Alpha Scylla, yet is quickly limited by the beast's webbing. As the Alpha Scylla approaches Minilla and plans to kill him, Minilla shouts out for his dad, who is dozing close to the red lake. Godzilla hears Minilla's cries, and heads to his salvage. The weather conditions control explore starts and is fruitful, making the temperatures on the island drop radically as snow falls. With Godzilla doing combating the Alpha Scylla, the researchers utilize the chance to get away from on a pontoon. the Alpha Scylla figures out how to twisted one of Godzilla's eyes and trap him in webbing, yet before he can complete him, Minilla acts the hero. Together, Minilla and Godzilla utilize their nuclear breath to set the Alpha Scylla burning and rout him. With the island starting to freeze solid, Godzilla and Minilla head for the sea, yet Minilla falls into the snow and starts nodding off. Reluctant to leave his child, Godzilla pivots and embraces Minilla in the snow, as they fall into hibernation together. The researchers are safeguarded by a Ruler chopper, lastly abandon Soul Island.

CHAPTER 7

Rodan The Fire Demon

I t is December 26, 2025. Mark Russell returns to his better half's grave, lamenting for her, since he actually had love for a large number of her definitive reclamation. Mark then gets called into a Titan fight to examine what is happening. Ends up, Rodan constrained the previous Titan living in Mount Fuji; Yamata no Orochi. Orochi took a stab at utilizing its sonic shriek, however Rodan cut it not long from now by a whirlwind wind. Rodan, then, at that point, cut off one of Orochi's head with a thunderbolt and skewered directly through Orochi by flying as high as possible out of sight and barrel-moving down the sky, similar to a blazing drill. The seriously injured eight-headed mythical serpent heads into the sea, where it can rest to recuperate or pass on. Rodan thunders triumphant as he moves down into the well of lava. Mark meets Specialists Ilene Andrews and Nathan Lind, who both headed back dependent upon the surface to research what was happening. After an evaluation, they figured out nobody really kicked the bucket, because of the Titans battling in a far off region of the mountain, yet many were as yet injured. With the control lattice at long last on, Imprint was feeling quite a bit better to see Rodan contained once more. Mark asked where Godzilla was, and Nathan let him know that Godzilla was at the Empty Earth, managing a lot greater things there; a goliath torrential slide happened, while Godzilla was wandering down to the Empty Earth, and Godzilla is attempting search for any enduring Titans in the rubble. Mark gradually gestured his head, while leaving. Ilene takes one glance at Nathan and shakes her head to him, then leaves.

In the mean time, Alan Jonah has been impelling another arrangement since the occasions of 2019. He got tests from the Empty Earth subsequent to capturing a HEAV. He was reproducing the Arachno-Paws and transforming them into another species called Meganulon, being more similar to dragonflies with monster hooks. Since the Meganulon were a lot more modest, just at around 2.5 meters long, Jonah slipped them into the hot volcanic Titan zone, to destroy the wires and pinion wheels of the regulation matrix and shut it down for good, yet not prior to killing some Ruler faculty.

Before this, Imprint gets together with Portage Brody, a Naval force Master Bomb Defuser and Military Sergeant. He let them know how a ton of things changed beginning around 2014, and has resigned for a long time beginning around 2014, yet is presently back in the field with a mended foot now, and presently being essential for Ruler's faculty. Rick Stanton and Sam Coleman likewise get together with Imprint, saying "It's definitely been too long," and "How's it going, man?" Imprint puts on a little grin all over, and goes to work and it we're hoping to ask what. Rick says that Rodan became essentially taller, from being 47 meters to being 62 meters. Rick guesses that the more new magma for Rodan is supercharging him essentially, giving him 15 meters of more level. Out of nowhere, Sam sees that the regulation framework has been closed down in some way. The Meganulon complete the process of biting on the ropes and deactivates the regulation network. All the fight and the commotion pesters Rodan, who stops these bugs. Rodan breaks out of Mt. Fuji and takes off high out of sight, with just a solitary supersonic dash of wind being abandoned by him. Nonetheless, one enduring Meganulon starts to take care of off on the serious intensity and radiation from

GODZILLA B.C.E

Mt. Fuji, and it itself becomes supercharged and begins to quickly change.

In the interim, Imprint is so befuddled about what coincidentally forded, told him not to stress. A group are inside the regulation zone to fix the framework. In any case, with statics in their radios, they hear a boisterous shriek inside and their cams show that they're being eaten by a goliath winged bug like Titan. Ruler haven't seen a Titan like this as a general rule, so they chose to give the Titan superspecies name "Titanus Megaguirus," named after a bug god in Japanese legends. Ilene and Nathan likewise assemble and see what is happening, and see the spring of gushing lava thundering. Ruler accumulated their Ospreys to have the work force and regular people close by to withdraw, as Mt. Fuji begins to eject without precedent for 1,000 years. 25 individuals kicked the bucket from the emission, the majority of them from the pyroclastic stream that immersed one Osprey.

Ruler sends warrior jets, labeled "Red Group" to put down Megaguirus for good, while containing Rodan back to a close by fountain of liquid magma. While Rodan can really have the option to be quelled, Megaguirus is "the dragonfly identical to the Skullcrawler," having the option to continue to move after serious wounds, because of its hereditary inundations and changes affecting its long for food and obliteration, meaning Ruler needs to put it down for good. In the wake of finding the Megaguirus to Tokyo Sound, they utilized similar strategies they utilized on Rodan in 2019; bait it away from the central area and lead it to a close by Titan. While soaring very high over the Pacific, Rodan jumped out of the blue to face the monster bug, however not prior to tearing away a couple of planes, since they were standing out. Rodan attempted to skewer Megaguirus, however he missed her and Megaguirus figured out how to clutch his nose and clasp it shut. Rodan attempts to shake it off, yet that detached a piece of his lower jaw and Rodan takes off and thunders in torment. Megaguirus keeps on chasing after the warrior jets, with them sending off their rockets into the bug. Be that as it may, Rodan lances Megaguirus into the sea where the two have a short fight in the sea until both fly out, with Rodan getting his magma burnt out, and Megaguirus having less mobility in water. The two unite on Osaka, where they hook and cut at one another, with Megaguirus slicing through his skin with her pincer, and Rodan countering with a cut to Megaguirus' eye. The fight closes with Megaguirus cutting Rodan with her back tail and decommissioning him. Rodan falls vulnerably as he watches the dragonfly sovereign fly away.

Mark gets together with English Lieutenant Henry James Gordon, and lets him know that projections show Megaguirus is going into London. Gordon got it, requesting regular folks to withdraw and tanks to be gotten up in a position firearm Megaguirus down. With Megaguirus at long last showing up in the city, the English Military open fire. With Megaguirus obliterating and killing the vast majority of the tactical powers with her savage strength and sheer size, as well as her double laser breath, a pillar which Nathan (who was at the scene) made sense of that it filled in as a goliath laser shaft from her mouth. Just Gordon and a couple of others endure her assault, as they saw that she constructed a home at the core of London. Sergeant Brody gets together with Lieutenant Gordon, and depicts an arrangement that the US military attempted in 2014 against the MUTOs. Before adequately long, Megaguirus additionally laid eggs to overwhelm the city to increase with its posterity. Brody intends to bomb the home while sleeping, with the help of Gordon, Ruler and the English Military.

The military arranged to send off a Radiance bounce onto the home, with Brody and Gordon going about as Mission Managers. At the point when they show up just mostly down the leap, Rodan appears with them a plunges down leaving a shockwave that killed or harmed many individuals. Brody, Gordon and a couple of others are as yet alive, with them figuring out how to initiate their parachutes, as Rodan combined on Megaguirus, with the previous utilizing a fire breath thunder to shred her eggs to pieces. Megaguirus, angered, begins to fight around with Rodan. Megaguirus overwhelms Rodan, with her going to convey the completing blow. Nonetheless, the people utilize the bomb that they planned to use to explode the home, as a method for diverting Megaguirus and delay for Rodan to get back up. In this way, they sent off the bomb through a gun which made Megaguirus yell in irritation, and pursued the flying corps. This, nonetheless, offered Rodan, the chance to get Megaguirus by the neck and crash into the ground. Rodan conveys the completing blow, the drill run and Megaguirus is left with an opening in her waist and passes on from blood misfortune. Rodan, being injured, retreats to a close by well of lava to recuperate, as the people watch him withdraw, and they celebrate triumph.

CHAPTER 8

Mothra Queen Of The Monsters

Colonel Bruce Baxter of Ruler's U.N. branch is looking at the Mothra egg that has been latent for the beyond 10 years as of recently, when it at last begins to beat yellow light. Baxter sees the hatchling rise up out of her egg and out of dread, she goes after the tactical faculty, and keeping in mind that not killing anybody, she abandons a path of obliteration and breaks out into ocean. Meanwhile, Madison Russell got a new line of work in a Burger Lord cheap food carport. She worked close by her companion, Josh Valentine, as Imprint Russell has accomplices in Ruler, Dr. Michael Sun and Nicholas Tatopoulos. They assemble around a chrysalis of

Mothra, while getting news that Godzilla is at present laying lethargic, as he has encountered a ruthless fight in the Empty Earth, subsequent to attempting to contain temperamental Titans, which nearly killed him. Mothra would need to take over for him, as Kong is still generally dealing with different circumstances in the Empty Earth, for example, the Foetodon populace outgrowing control and showing his child the methods of a hero.

In the mean time, the Stenz siblings, William and Alexander, need to find Alan Jonah again, as he continues to go free. He gets the help from Colonel Baxter and Specialist Kyle Connor to attempt to find him. Meanwhile, the Stenz siblings, in which they caught two of the wanderers from Zenith, Ernest Denham and Peter Englehorn, the remainder of which have not been caught at this point. They were grilled by the Stenz siblings, with the two saying that new beasts have been arising out of the Empty Earth and without Godzilla, they can outgrow control and attack the surface world.

In the mean time, Alan Jonah and Titan-Rise's bosses have captured a HEAV to go into the Empty Earth, wherein they showed up through an entry in the Cold, which was total inverse to the exploration camp, since it came from Antarctica. They figured out how to find a caught Titan in the Empty Earth Immense Ravine caught in a thick layer of ice, and they revealed uncovered hooks and began to establish explosives to stir the monster. Colonel Baxter and Specialist Connor was dispatched after the Empty Earth research camp announced sightings of the Titan-Rise eco-fear based oppressors, so they were sent with warriors to go with them. Nonetheless, when they showed up, it was past the point of no return. The bombs were set to detonate by means of explosion, and the second they showed up, the Ravine side began to disintegrate and fall, arousing a Titan who was not found by Ruler at this point.

Up on a superficial level, Bruce Baxter labels Imprint and Madison Russell, Ernest Denham and Peter Englehorn along for an examination after reports of a crevasse framing in the Empty Earth, and a dull and winged Titan uncovering itself in ice. They approach the fell mountainside and they question Denham and Englehorn whether they saw anything like the caught moth. Denham and Englehorn let them know they haven't seen anything like it. All at once, the chasm disintegrates as a goliath, winged and limbed Titan shows up. They all getaway as the Titan gets away from through the Empty Earth entry, up to the surface world. As they ventured out back to up to the surface, Nicholas Tatopoulos appears at caution them that the Titan had surfaced and had gone to obliterate New York City.

Mothra likewise went to New York to attempt to stop the new Titan. Mothra utilized her new capacity, which was shooting superheated light bars from her wings, which consumed a little piece of the Titan's skin. The winged Titan released a molecule energy pillar from his mouth. Mothra avoided it, countering it with webbing to the head. She was going to end the coordinate with her stinger, until the Titan thumped her to the side utilizing his denticle-prepared last part. Mothra staggered to the ground, with the Titan arrival a hard impact utilizing his bar. Mothra had to withdraw, to mend her extreme wounds. The Titan could now start his frenzy on New York City.

At the point when Ruler had recollected that Godzilla is as yet recuperating after a fierce fight in the Empty Earth, and with different Titans in hibernation, they were ill-fated for the present, until a brilliant light sparkled overhead, close to their base Palace Bravo. It was Mothra, the Sovereign radiating her God Beams. They looked into in wonderment, as they figured out that the radio waves radiated from her were really a coded message to ship off the people. She let them know that the Titan had a name; Dagahra, a name in which got from an adjoining island from Skull Island. The name of the island is Newborn child Island, which its tempest is solid to such an extent that the flows drive the explorer to Skull Island all things considered.

Mothra landed and drifted in the huge ocean of the Bermuda Triangle. The coded message tells them "You really want to see." Bruce, Imprint and Specialist Connor got on a MACV (Ruler Elevated Battle Vehicle), designed from the HEAVs, to pursue Mothra. Going through the enormous tempest of Newborn child Island, they demonstrated the veracity of a place that is known for magnificence, with creatures they have never seen; a residing turtle skeleton, bioluminescent moths, a monster dark ocean mite, as well as others an unfathomable number.

When they got off, they see that there is one more moth in sight, lying in rest. It was dark, had morn horns on its head, and had a red-yellow example on its wings, instead of the blue-green-orange example on Mothra. Connor lets his mates know that it seems to be a bat. Bruce Baxter advises Imprint Russell to refer to it as "Battra" by its normal name, and "Titanus Batora" by its Titan assignment, to make it likened to Mothra. Mark lets them know that it sounded truly cool, yet before they could talk any further, an uproarious screech reverberated through the shore. Battra got up, in the wake of being snoozing for a considerable length of time, as Mothra's twin sibling, to assist Mothra with warding off Dagahra, when she made sense of the circumstance.

When getting through the tempest again to go head to head against Dagahra, Bruce advises Ruler and solicitations to send reinforcement. Dagahra, in the mean time, had gotten done with destroying New York City and advanced toward Toronto, where Mothra and Battra met on him, and multiplied labeled him. Mothra utilized her light shafts to consume Dagahra's skin, with Battra releasing his purple crystal radiates at the winged reptile. Rankled, Dagahra began to pursue them, with Mothra and Battra drawing Dagahra to The Vortex in the Atlantic Sea. They dove into the water, and capably explored through the breaks of the Earth to advance toward the middle. Be that as it may, Mothra was gotten by her wing, however Dagahra's prehensile tail. Battra caused Dagahra to drain out of his tail immediately, permitting Mothra and Battra to escape until further notice.

Bruce and Imprint, who were pursuing them with their MACV, barely tried not to collide with Dagahra, when they made a sharp right transform into The Vortex's passage framework. Their reinforcement has at long last shown up, with many MACVs, terminating their Sort 96 Counter-Pinnacle Rockets at the monster. Dagahra, being dazed, turned their consideration towards the MACVs unit, and when they penetrated through the Empty Earth, they ended up before an electric web set up by Battra and Mothra, which made every one of them make sharp turns in a flash, and made some accident or perplex. Bruce and Imprint's MACV were going to crash, until Specialist Connor hauled them out, before they could collide with the wall. Dagahra, luckily, was sufficiently unfortunate to be trapped in the monster web and be tased by Battra's crystal power. Nonetheless, he immediately tore through the webbing and began to batter at the two bugs, rapidly overwhelming them, with Dagahra detaching half of Battra's left wing.

Bruce advised the excess group to focus on Dagahra's eyes and ears. They did as such, and Dagahra staggered to the floor of the Empty Earth. Mothra and Battra pulled out their stingers in their midsection, and handled the killing blow on Dagahra's head. They had won. Earth has been saved again, yet not by Godzilla, but rather by the force of Mothra and Battra. Mothra and Battra flew out of The Vortex and went directly towards the dusk, with the leftover MACVs sticking to this same pattern.

CHAPTER 9

Gamara The Great

A boat conveying plutonium slams into a drifting atoll off the eastern shore of the Philippines, one of numerous occurrences happening all through the area. As the odd development approaches Japan, a group of researchers finds orihalcum special necklaces and a stone chunk canvassed in Etrurian runes on the atoll. During the examination, the atoll unexpectedly tremors, obliterating the piece and tossing the researchers into the sea. One individual from the group, Imprint Russell, sees the eye and tusk of a monster turtle.

In the mean time, Madison Russell, presently a Ruler junior specialist, researches a town in the Goto Archipelago purportedly went after by a "goliath bird". While Madison is at first doubtful of the cases, she is frightened after finding human remaining parts in a monster bird pellet. Investigating the close by woods, her group experiences and afterward effectively forestalls three bird-like animals from going after another town. To forestall further assaults, Nagamine consents to help the public authority in catching the goliath birds. The animals are tricked to the MetLife Football Arena, where two of the three are effectively caught. The last one departures to Jersey City, where it is killed by the goliath turtle experienced by Imprint and the researchers. The excess birds get away from before the turtle arrives at the arena.

In the wake of deciphering the runes, Imprint clarifies for Madison and her companions, Aaron Knight and Fred Eddison, that the goliath turtle is assigned Titanus Gamera and the birds are Titanus Gyaos. At the point when Aaron contacts one of the stone talismans, he coincidentally frames an otherworldly bond with Gamera. Aaron additionally attempts to persuade the public authority that the Gyaos are the genuine danger, yet they stay zeroed in on Gamera because of the obliteration that he caused.

Presently cooperating to explore the animals, Aaron, Fred, Madison and one more companion of hers, Josh, witness another Gyaos assault at Mount Washington. Aaron and Fred are almost killed, yet

GODZILLA B.C.E

Gamera shows up so as to save them and kills another Gyaos. The last Gyaos, in any case, get away. In the mean time, Aaron finds that he experiences similar injuries and weakness as Gamera because of their common bond. At Mount Washington, she observes a tactical negative mark against Gamera. The assault draws in the last Gyaos to the scene, where it shockingly wounds Gamera and powers the turtle to withdraw into the sea. All the while, Aaron experiences a comparable injury and drops from the aggravation. Mark visits him at the medical clinic where Aaron falls into a trance like state subsequent to saying that she and Gamera should rest.

In the wake of finding antiquated relics, Madison and Fred discover that the Gamera was made by the Kong species some time in the past, against Godzilla, during the Titan war. Beginning of Gyaos stayed obscure, yet estimated that it was a subordinate animal varieties from Rodan, maybe the Kongs involving it as a final desperate attempt to stop Godzilla, just for them to self-isolate into the Empty Earth. They approach Aaron with this data, making sense of that the occurrence at Mount Washington shows that Aaron is in a profound way connected with Gamera.

With Gamera recuperating in the sea, the last Gyaos becomes unrestrained, turning into a Super Gyaos. The animal goes after New York City, making numerous regular citizen setbacks and inciting the public authority center around Gyaos rather than Gamera. Endeavors to kill Gyaos end in disappointment and it fabricates a home in the remains of the World Exchange Place.

After arousing from her rest, Aaron cautions the others that Gamera has recuperated and will go after Gyaos. Gamera gets Gyaos off guard, its home and eggs. A huge air fight results and Aaron, Fred, Madison, and Josh follow intently in a helicopter. At first, Gyaos overwhelms Gamera, yet Aaron utilizes his otherworldly energy to resuscitate Gamera, who kills Gyaos. Gamera, subsequent to utilizing his bond with Aaron to recuperate him, sets him free from their security and gets back to the ocean. While Madison and Josh foresee the likelihood that Gyaos or different dangers might emerge, Aaron expresses that Gamera will return assuming that occurs.

CHAPTER 10

New Chapter

As Godzilla swims through his oceanic territory, he witnesses a battle between the United States Coast Guard and Scylla near Savannah, Georgia. Godzilla recognizes Scylla as a Titan who earlier submitted to him, but realizes that she has become hungry and restless and is trying to obtain a nuclear bomb resting on the seafloor for sustenance. Godzilla recognizes the warhead as a human invention and knows that if Scylla feeds on the weapon, it will explode and damage the land and sea. With Scylla unwilling to surrender her prize without a fight, Godzilla attacks her. Godzilla tackles Scylla, who spears her legs into his body and draws his blood. She extends her tentacles at Godzilla's face, but he shakes her off and sends her slamming into a cargo ship. The two Titans exchange roars before Scylla launches her tentacles at Godzilla's face once again. Godzilla stumbles backward into an electrical sign near several oil tanks, causing the former to spark and the latter to explode. Amid the flames, Godzilla finds himself behind Scylla and lunges at her, launching her into the air. Scylla crashes into the water and gets back to her feet, growling at Godzilla. As the humans lift the warhead onto a ship, Scylla finally retreats underwater. Godzilla knows that Scylla will outswim him and won't challenge him again anytime soon. However, he also understands that he is needed elsewhere.

Godzilla thinks about how the world has changed since King Ghidorah awoke, and that with his death, there are still imbalances in his territory as it seeks a new equilibrium. Godzilla takes in the water swirling around him, then makes his way to the Amazon River. Not long before, the many small lives of the reefs were in pain, but are now healing well. The "deep singers" are breeding once more, which pleases Godzilla. Nearby, Behemoth is locked in battle with Amhuluk, who slashes off one of the Titan's massive tusks. Godzilla arrives in Behemoth's territory, which is also healing. However, Ghidorah caused too many of his Titan brethren to awake at once, putting them into conflict with one another. If this battle continues, the land will be further wounded. Behemoth strikes

Amhuluk with his other tusk, but Amhuluk retaliates with a punch that knocks Behemoth down. Amhuluk grabs Behemoth by the tusk and begins to drag him away, but Godzilla intervenes and throws Amhuluk. Amhuluk acknowledges Godzilla's status as "king" and leaves, while Behemoth stands up once more and wanders into his territory. Godzilla is tired, but his lair where he could rest and feed on the planet's energy is gone.

Godzilla swims under the sea and descends into the Hollow Earth to rest. Much has changed in Godzilla's lifetime. The land and seas have shifted, places that once burned are cold, and places that teemed with life are now abandoned. Godzilla reaches the place where his lair once stood, a place the humans had built for him. He remembers how Ishiro Serizawa had died for him here. As Godzilla descends a colossal staircase into his former lair, he realizes that something else is here now, something that should not be there. Godzilla is swarmed by a host of unfamiliar creatures, which he recognizes must have come from deeper within the Hollow Earth. As Godzilla fires his atomic breath, he perceives that the creatures seem to share a hive mind. Godzilla understands that the explosion that destroyed his lair must have breached the deeper parts of the Hollow Earth and that these creatures did not come alone. As predicted, the piranha-like creatures' massive leader bursts through a wall of rock and swims into Godzilla, biting down on his throat. Godzilla promptly tears the creature's skeleton from its flesh, and the hive mind shared by the creatures is destroyed. Godzilla incinerates the carcass with his atomic breath, and the creatures scatter. They will no longer emerge in this place once sacred to Godzilla. The energy from the Earth that Godzilla feeds on no longer collects in this place, so Godzilla must seek out a new source of nourishment.

Godzilla closes his eyes and shuts out the surrounding sounds, perceiving the winds that blow around the planet. In some places, the winds fold, like a place Godzilla once came to long ago. Godzilla may have called this place home, had a "rival" not driven him out of it. Godzilla surfaces and climbs up a cliff, drawn to the Moon which seems to call to him. Godzilla remembers how the ocean once divided his world, above and below. But now, they are one, and he sees the world anew. Godzilla sees a vision of Mothra as he remembers the sacrifice she made for him. Godzilla continues his search for a new home, led on by Mothra's gift of life. He decides to return to the place from which his rival had driven him, but senses something calling out in pain in the depths. Godzilla is compelled to defend his territory, so he goes to investigate its source. He sees many dead whales floating in the deep, and recognizes that they must have been killed by humans. He senses boats and oil, but also something else. He comes upon Na Kika, who is trapped within a massive net. She came here seeking solace and rest, only to be captured. Whatever has done this is violating the natural order. Godzilla tears Na Kika free. Godzilla realizes those who have done this have made war on the sea, and like Ghidorah, have come only to destroy for the sake of destruction. Godzilla fires his atomic breath at a nearby submarine and swims right through it, destroying the vessel. He surfaces near an oil drilling platform and is fired upon by helicopters. Some of the helicopters are shot down by Monarch jets, who were also assaulting the facility. Godzilla dives below the water and swims beneath the platform. Godzilla fires his atomic breath directly up at the platform, destroying it. He surfaces and roars victorious.

Godzilla continues swimming, needing his energy replenished. He swims through a tunnel into the Hollow Earth, then sharpens his dorsal fins on the rocks above him. He surfaces from beneath an ice shelf, and continues on his way, swimming past several humans as well as a Monarch submarine. Godzilla swims past the carcasses of many fallen Titans, and finally reaches his destination. He can sense that his rival is here as he comes ashore. He roars to signal his intentions, but to no reply. Suddenly, the nearby water swirls and Godzilla finds himself under attack by Tiamat. The serpentine Titan coils her body around Godzilla and pulls him underwater with a maelstrom, her scales cutting into him. He headbutts Tiamat in the mouth, but she expels a blinding acidic breath from her mouth into the surrounding water. Unable to see, Godzilla is still able to pinpoint his enemy's location with his other senses, and turns to face Tiamat as she tries to swim up behind him. Tiamat again coils around Godzilla and begins dragging him deeper and deeper underwater. Godzilla realizes that Tiamat is at her strongest in the deep, and that he must take the fight to land. Eventually, Tiamat pulls Godzilla through an underwater tunnel that leads to an air pocket. The Titans surface, Tiamat biting down on Godzilla's neck. Godzilla grabs Tiamat by the throat and uses his tail to smack her onto solid ground. He then stomps on her head repeatedly. Despite this, Tiamat defiantly roars at Godzilla. However, he responds with an even more fearsome roar that convinces Tiamat to back down. She then slithers back into the water and leaves. Godzilla continues deeper into the cavern, coming upon one of his old lairs, its walls adorned with paintings of him and his worshipers. Something is different though. His rival was not the same. Before Tiamat, there was another here. Godzilla sees the skull of a member of Kong's species and recognizes it as belonging to his rival.

GODZILLA B.C.E

Godzilla has found a new home, and will be able to rest soon. But first, he must call the other Titans to rest as well.

GODZILLA B.C.E

78

In this book is the conclusion for the Monsterverse series. There shall be many more journey's for these Kaiju titans in the future.